BAD MOUTH CHRISTOPHER

FLIZIT

Written and Illustrated by Bartholomew

CONCORDIA®

Publishing House
St. Louis

BAD MOUTH CHRISTOPHER

Printed in the United States of America

Library of Congress Cataloging in Publication Data

Bartholomew.
    Bad Mouth Christopher.

    SUMMARY: Confronted by a Bad Mouth Creature when he is sent to his room for swearing, Christopher turns to God for help.
    [1. Swearing—Fiction. 2. Conduct of life—Fiction] I. Title.
PZ7.B28128Bar   [E]   79-27658

ISBN 0-570-03482-5

*For my mother
with special thanks to Steve*

INTRODUCTION

"Sin" is one of those adult words children hesitate to say out loud. But they have their ideas of what it means. Early in life children learn the difference between right and wrong, and to them sin is the sum total of everything wrong. When children feel they have committed a real *sin,* it can be a devastating experience.

At about age seven, I overheard some older boys using profanity. I couldn't wait to repeat what I'd heard. Funny thing though, instead of feeling proud, I felt embarrassed; instead of feeling part of the crowd, I felt alone and frightened. My stomach tightened up, and my mouth became hot and dry. Soon my imagination took full control. I couldn't sleep—"things" were out there in the darkness waiting to do something dreadful to me. My smile faded and my head hung down. I had created a Bad Mouth Monster, and it *was me.*

Years later I realized that suffering from the "guilts" is not uncommon among children. When children do things they know are wrong, they often personify their fears—creating imaginary creatures to punish themselves.

This is a problem children shouldn't have to handle alone. They need not suffer from guilt. Learning that they will make mistakes, for nobody is perfect, is the first step. Next, knowing God is a loving and forgiving Father who loves and understands them, even when they don't always do what He wants them to do, is equally important. Finally, because of Jesus' sacrifice our sins are guaranteed to be forgiven. With this knowledge children will be relieved of unnecessary frightful worries.

As long as children are children they will fantasize. That is a healthy part of childhood. Writers frequently rely on past experiences for their work. This story is my fantasy—but it has a real-life application. My hope is that it will help some boy or girl to conquer the Bad Mouth Monster in them.

Bartholomew
Author/Illustrator

It just wasn't Christopher's day.
    EVERYTHING went wrong!
    He was late for school—lost his lunch money—
dropped the winning fly ball and his team lost—broke
his skateboard—And now, just when he was about to
go bike riding, it started to rain.
    "Sorry, Chris, you can't go now because it's rain-
ing," his mom called.

It just wasn't Christopher's day. And he had had enough!

"Miserable *&%$### weather!" Christopher shouted as he shook his fist at the sky and slammed his bicycle to the ground.

At dinner things didn't go any better. Of all the good things to eat, what did Christopher see before him?

LIMA BEANS!

"No lima beans, no cake," his father said sternly.
Christopher scooted the lima beans everywhere but in
his mouth. He offered them to Kazam, his dog, but even
he refused them.

Christopher sat thinking about all the things that had happened to him all day, and he got angrier and angrier, redder and redder, until he just exploded.
"Aw, rats. **%¢¢&," he shouted.

His mother gasped in disbelief, and his father ordered him to his room to wait for punishment.

"Phooey, ***¢&%$#? to you all," he mumbled to himself as he climbed the stairs to his room. "It's all your fault, you *&¢*%*** weather," he shouted to the rain. "And yours too, you *&¢¢¢$% dog. If you'd eaten the lima beans . . ."

KaB

KA BOOM!! the lights went out.

OOM

"What now?" Christopher shouted at the dark room.

He waited for his eyes to adjust to the darkness, then he stumbled into his room. Right in his way was a strange-looking creature.

Christopher sized the thing up. It was about his size, but it had two horns, bat wings, three toes on each foot, a long tail, and a terrible-looking mouth.

"What the ##%%&%&% are you?" Christopher asked.

"A Bad Mouth Creature," it answered.

"Did anybody ever tell you how ugly you are?" Christopher laughed.

"Did anybody ever tell you how ugly *you* are?" answered the Bad Mouth Creature.

Christopher didn't think that was funny one bit. "No," he huffed, "in fact, I've been told I was adorable . . . cute, even handsome . . . now, how about that?"

"Umm-mm," said the creature, fluttering to the top of the dresser and taking a comfortable position amid the clutter.

"They don't see you, or better, they don't *hear* you like I do," said the creature. "But we're partners, aren't we Christopher?"

"Look," shouted Christopher, getting angrier by degrees. "Why don't you get out of here you ¢$%$%#%!"

The Bad Mouth Creature laughed. "See what I mean," he said.

Christopher threw a shoe at the thing, but it ducked casually and laughed again. "I'm no partner of yours," Christopher yelled.

Christopher shouted and screamed, threw things and called the creature everything he could.

"Good, good, good," laughed the Bad Mouth Creature. "Keep it up."

Christopher slumped in the middle of the room, exhausted from his rage, and for the first time he looked at himself.

"Oh, no," he cried. "I'm beginning to look just like YOU. I'm becoming a Bad Mouth Creature."

"Yep," chuckled the creature as it swung from the light fixture. "All that ugliness on the inside is now coming out on the outside. In a little while you'll be just like me. Won't that be wonderful."

"No you #%&($%&$%)$*!" Christopher shouted,
and poof, his tail grew two feet longer.

The creature somersaulted to the bed and jumped for joy. Christopher sat in the middle of the floor feeling lost and alone. "I don't want to be ugly like this," he sobbed.

"But you are, you are," laughed the creature. "Now you look like you do on the inside."

"But I don't like myself like this," said Christopher.

"Oh," said the creature. "But you aren't thinking of changing are you?"

"Oh, I would if I could," Christopher sobbed.

Then Christopher remembered something. He hobbled over to the nightstand near his bed. The Bad Mouth Creature watched as Christopher pulled a book from the drawer.

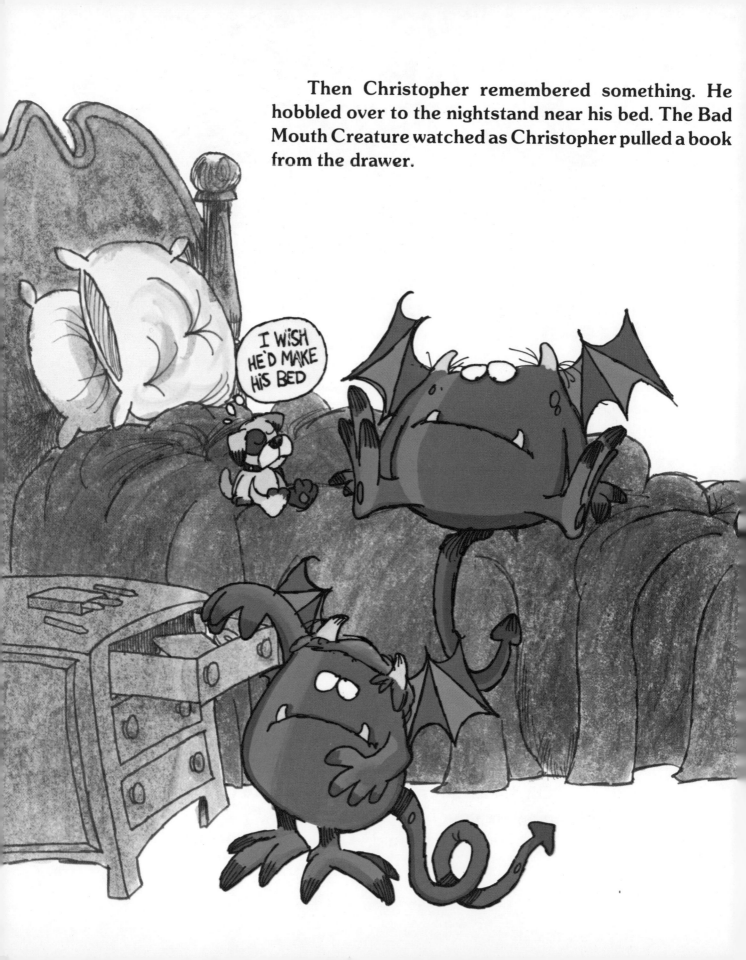

The creature huffed and puffed. "No, no, don't do that," he shouted. "You'll ruin everything I had planned for us. Don't change."

Christopher began to read and pray quietly. "Dear Lord, I'm not perfect, and I need your help in cleaning up my mouth. Please forgive me for bad-mouthing weather, which is your creation, my parents who love me, and my food for which I should be thankful. I ask forgiveness in the name of Jesus. Amen."

Suddenly, the lights came on. The room was back to normal, and the Bad Mouth Creature was gone. Even Christopher was back to his normal self again.

He heard his father coming up the stairs. Christopher knew why he was coming. "Oh . . . ," and he caught himself. He didn't swear. He smiled and whispered.

"I'm trying."